Little Quack's New Friend

by Lauren Thompson   *pictures by* Derek Anderson

SCHOLASTIC INC.
New York Toronto London Auckland Sydney
Mexico City New Delhi Hong Kong Buenos Aires

Mama Duck had five little ducklings, Widdle, Waddle, Piddle, Puddle, and Little Quack.
They all played together in the cool, shady pond.

One day, out jumped a teeny green frog.
"Ribbit, ribbit! I'm Little Ribbit!" he said. "Can I play?"

"No way," said Widdle. "You're too tiny!"
"And you're too green!" said Waddle.
"And you can't quack!" said Piddle.
"And you're a FROG!" said Puddle.
"That's okay!" said Little Quack. "*I want to play!*"

So—*quack, quack, ribbit, ribbit!*—
two little friends went off to play.

Over by the reeds Little Ribbit said, "Let's splash!"
"I love to splash!" said Little Quack.
Splishy, splosh!
"Can I splash with you?" asked Widdle.

"Sure!" said Little Ribbit.
Splishy, sploshy, splish! splashed three wet friends.

Over in the mud Little Ribbit said, "Let's squish!"
"We love to squish!" said Widdle and Little Quack.
Squashy, squooshy, squash!
"Can I squish with you?" asked Waddle.

"Of course!" said Little Ribbit.
Squashy, squooshy, squashy, squoosh!
squished four muddy friends.

Up on the log Little Ribbit said, "Let's bounce!"
"We love to bounce!" said Widdle, Waddle, and
Little Quack.
Boingo, poingo, boingo, poing!
"Can I bounce with you?" asked Piddle.

"Why not?" said Little Ribbit.
Boingo, poingo, boingo, poingo, boing!
bounced five hoppy friends.

Down by the lily pads Little Ribbit said,
"Let's dunk!"
"We love to dunk!" said Widdle, Waddle,
Piddle, and Little Quack.
Plunka, splunka, plunka, splunka, plunk!
"Can I dunk with you?" asked Puddle.

"Come on over!" said Little Ribbit.
Plunka, splunka, plunka, splunka, plunka, splunk!
dunked six bottoms-up friends.

Then Widdle said to Little Ribbit, "You know what? It's okay if you're tiny!"
"And it's okay if you're green!" said Waddle.
"And it's okay if you can't quack!" said Piddle.
"And it's okay if you're a FROG!" said Puddle.
"We *all* like to play!" said Little Quack.

Then—*splishy, sploshy, squashy, squooshy, poingo, boingo, plunka, splunka!*—how they played!

"Hooray for Little Ribbit,
our *ribbitty* new friend!"

**To Owen, our *plunka*,
splunka duckling!**
—L. T.

**For Ethan, Jonah,
Justin, and Kaden**
—D. A.

ISBN-13: 978-0-545-00381-0
ISBN-10: 0-545-00381-4

Text copyright © 2006 by Lauren Thompson
Illustrations copyright © 2006 by Derek Anderson
All rights reserved. Published by Scholastic Inc., 557 Broadway, New York, NY 10012,
by arrangement with Simon & Schuster Books for Young Readers, Simon & Schuster Children's Publishing Division.
SCHOLASTIC and associated logos are trademarks and/or registered trademarks of Scholastic Inc.

12 11 10 9 8 7 6 5 4 3 2   7 8 9 10 11/0

Printed in the U.S.A.   08
First Scholastic printing, January 2007

Book design by Greg Stadnyk
The text for this book is set in Stone Informal and 99.
The illustrations for this book are rendered in acrylic on Arches hot press watercolor paper.